tales of the WICKED CHILD

in Six Short Stories

By Jessica Feinberg

Author's Note

The stories and art in this book have been with me in one form or another since my teen years. Now I'm thrilled to share them and my love of storytelling, fairy tales, and folklore with all of you! Enjoy!

Thanks To:

My proofreading, feedback and support team:
Gemma, Daniel, and Jocelynne.

All the fairy tales and faeries that inspired me
and my grandma who read them to me.

To everyone at Bookmans including James and Kay!

FIRST EDITION DECEMBER 2019

Paperback ISBN: 978-1-64764-836-7
Kindle ASIN: B081XCVJ32

STORY ONE

The Origin of The Wicked Child

OR

She Who Ate More Than Half

Once upon a time, down by the old river, there lived a Wicked Child and her brother.

The Wicked Child had **wild black hair** that sprang from her head like the spines of a startled porcupine.

The Wicked Child had **crazy eyes** that darted every which way, taking in the world and planning wickedness for it.

The Wicked Child had a wide mouth that could curve into a **large wicked grin.**

And last, but certainly not least, The Wicked Child had a **brother.**

The Wicked Child's brother could pass for an ordinary boy, except he looked older and more worn than most children his age.

Long ago, The Wicked Child was a good, sweet child with a rosy, happy face.

Long ago, The Wicked Child was a good, sweet child with a kind smile and a voice full of laughter.

Long ago, The Wicked Child was a good, sweet child, BUT like many children she also had a insatiable craving for all things sweet and sugary.

One day a demon came to her in the form of an old lady.

The demon told her of the sweetest fruit.

The demon told her of the tastiest fruit.

The demon told her it was the most delicious fruit to be found in all the land.

The demon told her the fruit grew on a tall tree in the center of the large meadow.

But the children were not allowed to play in the large meadow!

Alas, the old lady demon was not done, and she also told the child, **"Anyone who eats the fruit will be wiser than wise and live longer than long!"**

The good child thought being wise and living long would be a good thing, even if she had to bend the rules a little. She was determined to get the fruit for her older brother whom she adored more than anyone in the world.

The next day she persuaded her brother to play in the large meadow. As soon as they got there she climbed into the tall tree.

Up and up and up she climbed...

And there it was! A fruit that shone red in the sun - like a perfect apple - yet held the shape of a pear and bore the leaves of a banana.

There was only one fruit in the tree so the good child plucked it and began to climb down.

Then she stopped. The fruit was so tempting and so mouthwatering... perhaps she could split it with her brother rather than giving him the whole thing!

That way, she reasoned, they could be wise and live long together. She could have her half now as the climb was SO very tiring.

And so, the child ate half the fruit.

She started climbing down again, then stopped. Her brother did not know of the fruit. She could eat it all!

She could become wiser than wise and live longer than long! She would, of course, use these talents to watch over her brother. She could make sure they had the best of best lives that could be had! She told herself this would be all the better!

And so the child ate the rest of the fruit.

Suddenly the leaves of the tree shook, and a larger than large green serpent slithered into view. "Foolish, greedy wicked child!" cried the serpent, "You have stolen my magical fruit!" With that the serpent bit her and both fell from the tree with a loud **THUMP ... THUMP!**

Her brother rushed to help, and stabbed the serpent with his hunting dagger - **once, twice, three** times! As it died the serpent hissed, "**A curse! A curse on you both!**"

The brother cut off the serpent's head, but alas! The venom was already running deep into the good sweet child's veins and it made her as wicked as wicked could be! The curse wove itself around her and her brother, invisibly working its evil magic.

The Wicked Child instructed her brother to cut off the serpent's rattle tail for her to play with and from then on she did only wicked upon wicked things.

To this day, many a mother in those parts still frightens her children with warnings like,

"Should ye hear the snake's rattle, run on home as fast as you can, for The Wicked Child's evil magic is at work!"

STORY TWO

The Witch's Curse

One day, when The Wicked Child was four and three years of age, she called to her brother, "Do you love me dearly brother?" And her brother answered as he always did, "Always darling sister!"

She asked again, **"Always upon always and forever upon forever?"** And her brother replied, **"Always upon always and forever upon forever!"**

Then The Wicked Child took his hand in hers and said, **"Then let us go out and make some mischief!"**

There was an old woman in the woods called the Weather Witch. People said she looked after the weather of the kingdom, but the truth of the matter was that she was not a witch at all. In fact, she had no powers except perhaps the power to inflict her bad mood upon others.

Still, people talked their talks and rumored their rumors! No one was brave enough to cross her - lest she send lighting down on their homes or cause their crops to dry up and die.

That morning The Wicked Child and her brother walked through the woods behind the river, down near where the old weather witch lived. And 'lo, the children saw a messenger making his way cautiously up the woodland path!

What an opportunity for trouble! Quick as anything, The Wicked Child shook her snake's-tail rattle all about and around herself and her brother. In the blink of an eye, she and her brother appeared to be two rosy, innocent, good children!

They ran up to the messenger and called out, "**Tell us, tell us, tell us please! Where are you going so deep in the woods?**"

The messenger, very surprised by the children, stammered, "I-I'm delivering an invitation from the King".

And, drawing himself up a bit (for they were only children, even in such a scary part of the woods) he continued, "The beautiful baby Princess Daffodil has just come into the world, you know, and I am sent to invite each and everyone to the celebration!"

The Wicked Child winked and blinked at her brother and turned big sad eyes upon the messenger. "Oh please good sir, if you mean to invite the old woman who lives in the cottage down this road, I must beg you not to!"

And her brother added, "Oh, please don't! She's our old Granny and she's very sick! If she got an invitation to the Palace she would see it as her duty and try to go! She might get even sicker yet and- and- " He broke off and both the children began to cry.

The messenger, quite taken aback, quickly sought to stop their tears, "Fear not children, if it is for the best I will not deliver an invitation to your Granny."

"Oh, what a kind man you are!" Cried the children, beaming at him through their tears.

As the messenger went on his way, he thought he heard a strange sound behind him, like that of a baby's rattle. He paid it no mind, for truthfully, he was rather glad not to have to venture farther into the woods. He had heard a good many scary stories about the old woman there. Rightfully so, the messenger would soon find.

A few days after the events described above, the celebration of the baby Princess Daffodil was held. Oh! The people of the River Kingdom had not seen such a gathering in a good many years!

Everyone ate and ate and talked and talked and laughed and laughed and then laughed some more, for good measure. They admired baby Princess Daffy a great deal too, of course, and so all was merry and all was good.

Suddenly, halfway past the fifth hour of celebration, there was a great bang and the huge doors of the banquet hall flew open. In stalked the bent, twisted, old Weather Witch!

She pointed a wrinkled, crooked finger at the King and cried out, "How dare ye?! How dare ye?! You make merry and carry on while I toil away in the woods! My back aches! For your clear skies, I toil hard to chase the storm clouds away!"

The King stared at her in alarm, for he had thought her invited.

Nearby, the royal messenger turned pale under his nice, bright tunic and stammered, "B-but... your grandchildren said-"

"Grandchildren? What are you going on about?!" cried the old witch. "I have no grandchildren! Excuses shall not save you!"

The King sought to pacify the witch with apologies, but the Queen, angry that her celebration had been so disrupted, cried out that the witch should just leave them be! After all she was only an old hag, what could she do?

The witch, quick as a flash, was by the cradle! She waved her walking stick in the air and shouted,

"Clickity, rickity, snickity, black, bangy, wangy, thwiticky, thwack! I curse your daughter, you spoiled King and Queen! I curse her! I curse her! You'll see what I mean!"

The King cried out in distress,
"Oh witch, what have you done to our child?"

And the witch answered, "**She shall suffer misery and hardship and there is NOTHING you can do. You cannot protect her from my curse!**"

The King would not give up on his child. He told his wife that if the curse could not reach her, she would be safe.

And the King sent his daughter to the country to live with serving maids who would care for her and keep her always safe and happy. For surely, she would be safe where no people knew of her or could reach her.

But somewhere in the woods, down by the old river, The **Wicked Child was laughing.**

So time passed. Princess Daffodil grew from a child to a young woman. The old witch passed away, but The Wicked Child and her brother did not age or change, being trapped in the wicked curse as they were.

Left to do as they wished, the serving maids had made themselves out to be noble ladies and Princess Daffodil became their maid. She thought herself to be a poor girl taken in by the noble ladies and meant to spend her life serving them. Oh, how mean they were!

Morning, noon, and night they could be heard calling out, **"Daffy! Daffy! Where is my breakfast?"** And, "**Daffy! Sweep out the fireplace! Mop the floors! Alter this dress - you must have shrunk it in the wash!"**

They took all the fine things the King sent and Daffodil was left to wear rags.

They ate all the fine foods the King sent and Daffodil was left to eat the scraps.

They locked away all the toys and trinkets the King sent and Daffodil was left to draw in the dirt with a stick.

The King grew old and sad, and finally grew sick. He never visited his daughter. "She must be kept secret and safe from the curse!" He told himself and his wife as nineteen years slipped by.

One of the King's knights, who loved the King like a father, decided something must be done.

He set out to find the Princess and bring her back. She should be with her father when he is so sick, the knight thought - curse or no curse!

Should the King die, the Princess should know him and what a great King he was. After all, one day she would have to rule the Kingdom - curse or no curse!

The young Knight followed the secret messengers who were sent with food and gifts for the Princess.

He came to the cottage in the country where they lived. A young servant girl was mending clothes by the cottage door, she had dark eyes and hair of pale yellow.

She rose when he dismounted and said, "Oh, a Knight! You are a Knight, aren't you? I haven't seen one ever! I've always wanted to!" Then she turned red and curtsied deeply, adding quickly, "Forgive me, I've forgotten my place!"

The Knight smiled, for this girl was truly very pretty. "I've come to speak to the Princess."

"The Princess?" The girl looked puzzled. "It's only me and two noblewomen who live here."

"That cannot be, dear girl. I have seen the King's messengers bringing gifts for her here!"

"But there is no Princess here." The girl seemed quite sure of herself.

"There must be! Princess Daffodil was sent here many years ago-"

"T-That's my name," The girl cried in alarm. "But sir, you must be mistaken, I am no Princess!"

And then the Knight understood what had transpired. This beautiful (though perhaps in need of a wash) serving girl was actually Princess Daffodil!

He told her the truth and that he would take her back to the palace to see her father, the King. He wished to take the two serving maids and have them punished for their cruelty too.

But young Daffy would not hear of that. She said, "So much misery and hardship has come to me. I do not have the heart to wish it upon anyone else!"

And the Knight saw she was truly a good and kind Princess - curse or no curse!

Thus the Knight returned Princess Daffodil to the palace where the King was able to spend the last few months of his life with her. She eventually wed the Knight and they ruled over the Kingdom wisely for many years.

And so, The Wicked Child's evil was undone, for the Princess had learned the truth of the curse: The King's fear was why he had sent her away and why she had suffered misery and hardship.

In truth, no one has the power to control or shape your life unless you give it to them through your own fear.

But somewhere in the woods, down by the old river, The Wicked Child lived on. And she would be Wicked again.

STORY THREE

The Simple Minded King

OR

What Became of the Royal Messenger

As you may remember, the Royal Messenger was very distressed over the Princess Daffodil and the curse. He felt he was to blame because he did not deliver an invitation to the Weather Witch. He fled the Kingdom and traveled far into other lands.

He had many adventures and became something of a hero, eventually marrying a Princess of his own. They became King and Queen of The Kingdom at the Edge of the World and had three sons. This is the story of the three sons and, in particular, the youngest of those sons.

~

Once upon a time, in The Kingdom at the Edge of the World, there ruled a King and his three sons. The King was old and knew his time in the world would soon be over, so he called his three sons to him.

"One of you will have this kingdom to rule when I am gone." Said the King. "To determine which one of you it will be, I present you with a challenge."

The King turned to the oldest son who, being the oldest, had the right to try to claim the throne first.

"Get a ship and travel the sea until you find the Isle of the Golden Temple. Enter the temple and stay as long as you feel is necessary; then return and tell me what you have found there."

And so it was that the eldest of the three sons set out to find the temple. He sailed seven days and seven nights and at last came upon the Isle of the Golden Temple.

Hurriedly, he pulled his boat ashore and made for the temple, only to be confronted by a troll who seemed determined to keep him from entering. The Prince, however, had been trained well in the way of the sword and quickly decapitated the monster.

He entered the temple and then stood in silence for a moment. "Impossible!" He cried. Cursing his father, he returned angrily to his boat and sailed for home.

There was a great feast at the return of the first son. Afterwards the King asked him, **"Now my son, what is it you found in the temple?"**

The son replied in a rather irritated way, "There was nothing in the temple at all! I must say it was a very clever trick on your part - sending me all that way for nothing!"

At dawn it was announced that the first son would not be King.

~

The second brother set sail in the early morning hours - eager to prove his worth. He sailed for ten days and ten nights, 'til at last he found the Isle of the Golden Temple.

He made swiftly for the structure, only to be stopped by three trolls and a baby hydra!

He fought well and, within the hour, all the beasts lay dead at his feet.

Entering the temple, he saw what the first brother had seen: nothing. But the second son thought to himself that he be must be wise and not blinded by anger as his brother had been. He sat many minutes in the temple and at last set out for home.

A second feast was held, even larger than the first. As you can guess, the King asked his son what he had found in the temple.

> "It was simple," the son replied proudly. "The temple was filled with the dust of the earth that had blown inside. But if you want a more spiritual answer, it was filled with the spirits of things passed before."

At dawn it was announced the second son would not be King.

~

The last brother was considered simple-minded. His brothers laughed at him when he set off in an old rowboat, for they had made sure it was the only boat available to him. The youngest son did not mind, and he started rowing... and rowing.... and rowing... and rowing some more after that.

All this time the gods had been watching the prices tramp about their temple with interest and a little annoyance. "Our temple is too easy to reach," one of the gods said, **"it needs to be more of a challenge!"**

On his fifth day of rowing, the Young Prince encountered something unexpected: mountains. **Dead in his path was a mountain range, as if it had sprouted from the sea overnight!**

The Young Prince was not discouraged, for he was indeed a simple-minded lad, and as many know, simple-minded people cannot be discouraged as easily.

He broke his little boat apart and affixed it to his back with some rope (adventuring princes always carry rope - even simple-minded ones - just in case they need to tie up a wicked sorcerer). Then he began to climb... and climb... and climb.

When, at last, he made it over the mountains, the Young Prince was so tired he dropped down and slept on the sandy shore for two days. Upon waking, the Young Prince built a raft from the pieces of his boat and began rowing once again. **Two days later he came upon another unexpected difficulty: a massive whirlpool!**

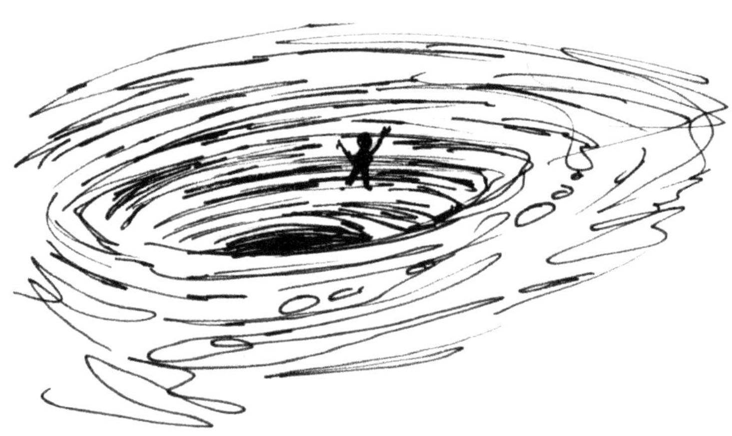

Though he held on for dear life, his raft was torn from him in the storm, and he lost all awareness of things that came to pass in the following days.

He awoke to find himself on the sandy shore of the Isle of the Golden Temple. **Perhaps the gods had taken pity on him at last!**

He knew not how much time had passed since he had left home. Time seemed to have left him behind. His thoughts on his father, he made quickly for the temple, but was faced at the gates with countless trolls and a giant hydra!

His sword had been torn from him in the whirlpool, but he was a simple-minded lad, and (of course) did not feel fear.

How long he fought, one could not say - one day or ten, it did not matter. At last the beasts lay dead at his feet.

Being simple-minded, he did not see them as bad creatures. So, before entering the temple, he spent much time and effort burying every one of the trolls AND the hydra (including all its heads).

At last, the Young Prince climbed the steps to the temple and entered. **He sat a long time inside.**

Then he built himself a raft from trees on the island, sent a prayer of thanks to the gods, and set sail for home.

The whirlpool and mountains seemed to have vanished as quickly as they had appeared, and he made good time. Five days paddling saw him reaching the shores of home.

No feast was held on his return, for his father was dying. The King called his youngest son to his bedside and asked what he had found in the temple.

"Why father," said the simple-minded son. "**What I found in the temple was simply the satisfaction of having made the journey.**"

~

The Young Prince was crowned King, and his father died only a few months after. Being a kind and generous lad, he shared his kingdom with his brothers and the three ruled happily. The youngest son, however, was always a favorite with the people of the kingdom, and he was known far and wide by many as "The Simple Minded King."

For he knew a simple truth: sometimes enjoying your life matters more than how long it takes you to get somewhere.

STORY FOUR

What the Three Princesses Found

As time passed in the Kingdom at the Edge of the World, the three sons all married and had children.

Two of them had sons who grew up to rule the kingdom together, and one had a daughter. She was an impossible child!

At the age of seventeen she was an adventuresome young woman. She set out to explore the world. Helping many folk in her journeys, she became known far and wide for her kind heart and brave spirit. But those are other stories. This is the tale of what happened after her adventures.

Eventually she settled down, marrying a young King. This King, by coincidence, was the son of Princess Daffodil and the Young Knight (who had passed into the next world by this time).

And so, the kingdom she became the Queen of was the very one in which The Wicked Child still lived.

What she and her husband wanted more than anything in the world was a child of their own, but they didn't seem to be able to have one. And yes, this does seem to be a common problem with Kings and Queens of that era.

One day the King was hunting in the forest (which is what kings do when they are not doing boring paperwork like decrees and taxes) and he chanced upon a fairy who was trapped beneath a fallen tree. The King dismounted and, using his sword for leverage, freed her.

Unknown to the King, the fairy had once been a kind, good fairy, but she had heard the sound of The Wicked Child's rattle. The sound lured her into the forest where the tree fell upon her. Trapped there for so long, she had become twisted and bitter.

Jumping to her feet, the fairy sneered at the King.

"Curse ye! Curse ye! For I am a twisted and dark creature! As it is the fairy law, I must grant you your greatest wish, but with it you will receive an even greater curse!"

The King rode with all speed back to the castle, but everything seemed as before and he sighed in relief. Perhaps the fairy had only been making an idle threat out of spite.

~

A year later the Queen gave birth to not one, but three beautiful daughters. Unfortunately, the Queen did not survive the birth. With her last words she asked the King to care for the babies and never let anyone take them away.

As he grieved over the cradles of his children, the King heard a noise at the window. Turning, he saw the fairy he had saved in the forest the year before.

"Here is thy greatest wish my King." She sneered. "Are you happy now? You shall have the three most beautiful and vain daughters in the land!" Laughing, she vanished as quickly as she had come.

The King was caught in a wave of despair and he knew not what to do.

Suddenly, he heard a little voice calling out to him. "Fear not King, for I will help you!"

Looking, again, to the window, the King perceived another fairy perched there - one who had managed to avoid The Wicked Child, which was rare in those parts.

"Your daughters shall not be completely vain so long as you care for them and teach them well, for no evil spirit can ever change that which is born in love."

Years passed, and the three Princesses grew more beautiful by the day. As their beauty grew, the King worried more and more. He feared they would become vain. He feared someone would come to take them away from him. They must be protected, it was his wife's dying wish.

On their sixth birthday, (for they were all born on the same day) he made an announcement. The Princesses were to be sent away to live in a cottage deep within the forest (not far from where the old Weather Witch had lived many, many years before).

They were given only one maid to serve them and were forbidden to wander far.

At first the Princesses were distressed at their change in lifestyle, but the King often came to visit and always brought fine gifts, so they were content.

~

One dark and particularly stormy night, a Prince was traveling a little-used road close to the forest in which the Princesses lived. The Prince's coach was ill-equipped for the horrible condition of the road and it soon lost a wheel.

Being the adventurous sort, (as many Princes are due to how boring life in a castle is) he continued his journey on a lone horse.

He did not know that somewhere in that old forest, down by an old river, lived a Wicked Child... and she knew of him and was working her wicked ways.

Upon the wind came a strange rattling sound the Prince could not identify.

Lightning crashed, thunder rumbled, and suddenly bandits sprang forth and surrounded the Prince. Though he fought bravely, his horse was slain from under him and he was wounded badly.

Fleeing into the forest, he ran until he was on the edge of death. Yet as luck (or perhaps that one good fairy) would have it, he happened upon the cottage of the three Princesses.

Stumbling to the door, the Prince raised his hand to knock, but could not find the energy to do so. He fell against the door, then slid to the ground, unconscious!

Inside the cottage, the King and Princesses were sitting around the fire. The youngest Princess (by a few moments) was reading poetry aloud. All felt quite safe and glad to be so cozy on such a stormy night.

Suddenly they heard a mighty THUMP against the door!

The eldest Princess sat up straight in her chair, crying out in alarm "Oh, father! What can that be?"

“Fear not.” The King told his daughters, “It is just a branch fallen against the door, I shall put it right.”

The Youngest Princess, concerned for her father’s safety, hurried after him to the door.

The King and his daughter opened the door and were, at first, struck so hard by wind and rain they could not see anything.

Upon recovering her senses, the Youngest Princess cried out in alarm, grabbing her father’s arm.

“Oh father, a man lies upon our doorstep! Is he dead?”

Hearing her cry, the other two Princesses (their curiosity overcoming their fright) ran to the door where their younger sister was bent over the Prince.

The King simply stood there, stunned, thoughts racing though his head. For all his careful planning... all his work... he could not let his daughters be taken from him by this man!

Now, perhaps a clever reader will begin to see the fairy's curse had worked itself more upon the King than his daughters. As we learned in an earlier tale, fear can be a terrible curse in itself, and fear out of love can twist the mind in mysterious ways.

Yet, the King had not been left without all sense and feeling. He knew he could not let this man die on his doorstep - no King could and still call himself a King. He had to quickly figure out what to do!

Pushing his daughters aside, the King hurriedly lifted the unconscious Prince and carried him into his chamber, closing the door behind him.

The King stayed up all night and cared for the Prince, bandaging his wounds and soothing his raging fever. By morning, he could tell the Prince would live but would need to stay in bed for several more weeks.

So he forbade his daughters from entering the room, lest they should look upon this man and take a liking to him. He would not even allow the maid inside!

As curious as the Princesses were, they would not disobey their father and so tried to go about life in a normal manner. The King did not return to his castle. He stayed in the forest to care for the Prince and watch over his daughters.

Now, this Prince was not only a brave young man, but also well-educated. So while the King sat with him, they talked much of the world and of life.

After many days, the King began to see the error of his ways. He was starting to love this prince almost as dearly as his own children, and knew he could not keep his daughters forever.

He thought if one of them ended up with the Prince he would be better off, for the Prince was a fine young man. So, the King came to the Prince with his eldest daughter.

"This is my daughter, Prince." He said "She is yours to marry with my blessing. Will you have her?"

The Prince looked upon the girl and saw she was truly the most beautiful maiden he had ever seen.

He replied "Kind King who has cared for me well, this young lady is very beautiful, yet I know her not. I will not marry a girl I do not know."

The King grew a little angry at this, though it was a wise remark, and said to the Prince, "If you would know my daughter, you may ask her just one question. Then decide if you will have her or not."

The Prince considered this, and said to the Eldest Princess, "Tomorrow when the sun rises, walk to the river, look into it, then return and tell me what you saw."

The next morning, the Eldest Princess walked down to the river and looked into it for a moment. Returning to the Prince, she said, **"I looked into the river and saw my own reflection and how beautiful I am."**

The Prince turned to the King and declared, "I cannot marry your daughter, she is vain and sees only her own beauty."

The King was very angry at this, but he brought the Middle Princess to the Prince saying, "Here is yet another daughter of mine, you may have her for a wife. Ask your question."

The Prince turned to the girl and said, "Tomorrow, when the sun rises, walk to the river and listen. Then return and tell me what you heard."

Early the next day, the Middle Princess walked down to the river and stood there for a long while; listening.

She then returned to the Prince and said, **"I listened by the river and heard all the insects and bugs mocking me, saying that I am not as beautiful as my sisters."**

The Prince turned to the King and declared, "I cannot marry your daughter, for she thinks only of how others are better than her."

The King was both angry and sad at this, but he brought the Youngest Princess to the Prince and said, "Here is my last daughter. Ask your question."

The Prince turned to the girl saying, "Tomorrow when the sun rises, walk to the river, stand there awhile, then come back and tell me how you felt."

Early the next morning, the Youngest Princess headed for the river. She wanted very much to marry the Prince. In truth, she had from the moment she'd found him at the door. But when she came back, she stood before the Prince with tears in her eyes.

She said hurriedly , **"I started down to the river, but found a wolf that had been hurt badly! He needs help, so I've only come back for some bandages!"** She turned to go saying **"I am sorry, I failed the task you gave me."**

The Prince turned to the King and said, "I shall marry this girl if she will have me! For she thinks of others before herself and is neither vain, nor selfish!"

And so, the Prince and the Youngest Princess were married and had a beautiful daughter. They ruled the Prince's Forest kingdom with great kindness and wisdom.

The King took his other two daughters back to the palace, leaving the cottage by the river empty... and the woods empty... save for The Wicked Child and her brother.

For still she lived on, and still, she went about her wicked ways and would for some time to come.

STORY FIVE

The Bird Who Flew Without Wings

One night, when The Wicked Child was seven and four years of age (for she did age so slowly), she said to her brother, "Do you love me dearly brother?" And her brother answered, "Always!" She asked, "Always upon always and forever upon forever?" And her brother replied, "Always upon always and forever upon forever!"

Then The Wicked Child took up his hand and looked into his eyes demanding, **"Then go out into the world and bring me back something sweet!"**

So The Wicked Child's brother (who was ten and seven years) went out into the dark woods. He wandered until he saw a cloaked traveler hurrying along the road with a bag from the market. He grinned to see someone out so late. Ah, such good luck!

The next morning The Wicked Child was sitting upon her doorstep eating a sticky bun - the bun which her brother had stolen from the traveler in the woods the night before.

Oh, how The Wicked Child loved sweets! She grinned and sang a funny little tune while eating.

“Hey, Hi! Oh My!
I’ve got a sticky bun!
Watch out passersby,
I am a tricky one!
Fe, fi,
I’ll put out your eye!
I’ve got a sticky bun!
Steer clear!
There’s trouble here!
Oh, aren’t I the lucky one?”

The Wicked Child was eating so hastily and so greedily that a bit of her Sticky Bun dropped to the ground. A nearby bird hopped over to peck at the tasty crumbs.

The Wicked Child grew angry (as wicked children do) that anyone else should have even a few crumbs of her tasty snack! She shook her rattle at the bird crying,

“You greedy, greedy, GREEDY bird! That was my sticky bun! I curse you!” And she stamped her foot three times. The poor bird fluttered off in great distress.

The bird had a nest with three baby birds in it, but when she returned to the nest, she found the smallest bird was missing. Though she flew round and round and over and over the land searching for her baby, she could not find the little bird. Whatever curse The Wicked Child had worked had sent the little bird far, far away.

This is the story of that little bird.

Once there was a little bird who lived in the highest of high mountains. The little bird had no mother or father that it could remember. The little bird had no companions at all, save for the clouds that floated past, but the little bird was happy.

On this high mountain there were many sharp upon sharp rocks. In fact, one could not walk about at all, only fly from landing spot to landing spot in-between the rocks. Yet the little bird was happy, for there was enough sky to fly round and round forever.

As the little bird grew, it began to take the sky and clouds and its life, in general, for granted.

Soon the little bird said to itself, "There is something in my life I am missing, I shall have to find it." And so, the little bird began to fly a little further down the mountain every day.

One day the little bird finally flew far enough down that it saw some other birds perched on a ledge, and it swooped in to land and talk with them.

To the little bird's surprise, it saw the other birds walked about using their legs and feet. The little bird did not know how to walk about like that, as it had never learned.

"What is that strange thing you do with your legs?" The little bird asked.

The other birds only laughed at the little bird and squawked, "Little bird can't walk, little bird can't walk!" Then they flew into the air, flapping their little wings hard. The sound of their laughter drifted back as they vanished from sight in the clouds.

The little bird sat and cried 'til a small voice called out, **"Don't cry, little bird."**

Looking around, the little bird saw another little bird with the smallest wings in the world (or at least the smallest it had ever seen).

The second little bird continued, "They are just jealous because you can fly so well. Tell me why you cannot walk."

The first little bird told the second little bird its story and the second little bird said, "Why I've had the exact opposite problem! I can walk miles, I can even swim and fish, but I cannot fly."

The two little birds spent much time together when one day it occurred to the first little bird to ask,

"If you cannot fly, than how did you get here and how do you get around?"

"I walked up the mountain," replied the second little bird with a sigh, "it took a long time to get here - the ground is so very far below!"

"Ground?" asked the first bird. "I do not understand, is not the whole world like this place?"

"Why, no!" laughed the second bird. "Have you never been below the clouds? Have you never seen the earth or sea?"

"Below the clouds?" Wondered the first little bird. "Please, can you take me?" For now, the first little bird was sure this "ground" place was what it had been looking for its whole life.

"What would you want to go to the ground for?" asked the second bird. "There's nothing down there, it's the up, up, up where the better places are!"

"That cannot be, for I have lived as high as anything and seen nothing better than clouds and sky and sharp upon sharp rocks."

"Maybe so..." said the second bird, but it did not really believe the first little bird at all. "I'll tell you what. I'll teach you how to walk on the ground below the clouds if you teach me how to fly up high."

The first little bird could see nothing wrong with this idea - both birds getting what they wanted - and so agreed.

Many months later, the birds were fed up with each other. The first little bird was angry because it still could not walk. It seemed to the bird that its legs were only made for pushing off into flight. They didn't bend in the right ways.

"This cannot be the place I am looking for," thought the little bird about the ground, "but I have been above and below, and now I have nowhere left to go."

The little bird had done its best to teach its new friend to fly, but there had been a problem: the second little bird was perfectly capable of learning to fly; it was just too afraid.

"Perhaps," the first bird mused, "my friend is afraid I am right and there is nothing above the clouds to find."

Knowing the thing which it looked for did not exist, the first little bird grew depressed and grumpy all the time, so the birds fought constantly.

One day they were sitting in the hot sand, having just had a fight. They sat, each thinking the other stupid, and feeling sorry for themselves.

Then there was a tremendous rumbling sound and a massive shadow fell across them (remember they were very little birds).

“This must be what I’ve been looking for!” The first little bird thought in innocent joy. “Something amazing will finally happen!”

A man got out of the carriage and looked at the birds. This frightened them.

“Flee!” They cried together, but neither would leave the other behind - they really did care for each other deep down - and so they were stuck since one couldn’t fly and one couldn’t run. This created a very comical picture! The man laughed and scooped them up in a net.

He took them on a long journey in cages, but the first little bird was happy. “I’m finally going to get there!” it cried (not really sure where “there” was, but it was somewhere).

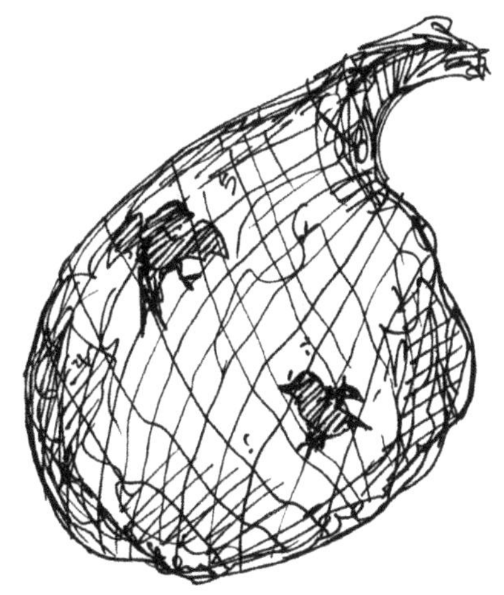

"Fool!" scolded the second bird. "This creature simply means to cook us for dinner!"

So the birds fought until the man took them to a place where there were many other creatures in cages.

Then the man did a vile, vile, thing - but people will do awful things for money! He cut the first little bird's wings and the second little bird's legs.

The birds cried out, but there was nothing they could do. They were put into a big cage where people would come and pay to laugh at a wingless bird trying to fly and a legless bird trying to walk.

The little birds cried and called, but to no avail. No one would help them. Slowly, the first little bird began to die, for it had no place to go, no faith left in the world and thus, no hope to keep it alive.

The second little bird kept itself alive and in good health, promising itself it would reach the land in the clouds as soon as it made its escape.

On the last night of the first little bird's life, it called to its friend, "Oh my friend! There is nothing above the clouds and nothing on the ground. There is nothing to live for!"

But the second little bird would not listen. It would not believe that. Suddenly, a mighty gust of wind swept the cage door open! The second little bird (who had learned to roll about and walk on the stumps of its legs) got quickly out of the cage, but the first little bird still lay dying.

The second little bird was now faced with a choice: leave behind its only friend and go to the higher and better place, or stay with a deceived, foolish bird 'til it died. The choice was made without second thought.

The little bird lay alone in the cage in the dark, without even enough energy to cry.

"Oh, what shall become of me?!" It thought, "What shall I do with nowhere to go when I die?"

"Oh, little bird!" called a soft voice. "There is still a place to go!"

Raising its head with the last of its energy, the little bird saw a beautiful creature with great white wings kneeling next to the cage.

"What kind of bird are you!?" it asked in wonder.

“I am an angel,” the creature answered. “I come to those who need faith and hope.”

“I have none, fair creature,” sighed the little bird. “I have been up. I have been down. I have been by the sea. I have been in the village. I have nowhere to go.”

"Poor Little bird," said the angel, "there is another direction you may go in, that is neither up nor down. That is the place where I flew here from."

"Can it be?" whispered the little bird. "But how will I find it? I am so tired! I cannot fly!"

"You must simply look here," the angel touched the little bird's heart. "As for the power to fly, you have it now as you always have."

The little bird looked quickly at its wings, but they had not grown back.

"How can I fly without wings!?"

"You can fly with your faith."

"What is faith?" the little bird asked.

"Why," the angel laughed "it was your very looking for something you knew was there; it was your very believing there was something better than what you knew."

The little bird closed its eyes and found its heart and its faith. When it opened its eyes, all was different.

"What happened?" it wondered in surprise.

"You are an angel too," the angel told little bird. "Come. Let us leave this place."

The little bird (now turned angel) and the angel flew out above the sea and the sand.

Soon the little bird saw its old friend rolling and stumbling towards the mountains. The little bird flew to its friend and cried out, "My friend! My friend! I have found the way to the better place!" But the second little bird would not listen.

It cried, "Be gone evil spirit, you only try to dissuade me from the path to the clouds."

The little bird started to cry, but the Angel comforted it. "Do not cry, my friend. Sometimes spirits need to discover things on their own. Some can take longer, harder paths to find their faith. Do not waste tears on your friend, for that bird left you for its own idea of happiness, but happiness can never mean more than the love of a friend."

Then the angel led the little bird to the better place.

In the morning, when the man looked into the cage, he could only stare in wonder. There were no birds inside, not the walking one, not the dying, flightless one.

Nothing but a pile of bright white feathers glowing brilliantly in the morning sunshine. But the cage, oh the cage, it had turned to solid gold!

Lying at the door to the cage was the walking bird, as dead as anything - for it had died the second it stepped out of the cage alone.

The man picked up the white feathers and saved them. He released the birds and other animals he had kept captive for entertainment and money.

He gave the walking bird a decent burial. Then he sold the big cage and took the money to help sick and injured people (and birds).

And on stormy winter nights around the fire, the man would sit and tell his children and after that, his grandchildren, the story of the little bird who flew without wings.

Meanwhile... somewhere in the woods, down by the old river, The Wicked Child lived on, and she would be Wicked again.

STORY SIX

What Became of the Wicked Child

The Wicked Child, in all her wicked wisdom, did not know everything. She did not know her brother had not stolen the sticky bun which she had so enjoyed. He had meant to, for sure he had, but when he glimpsed the stranger's face on the road that dark night... she had been beautiful.

She was, as chance would have it, the great granddaughter of Princess Daffy. She had inherited her great grandmother's spirit and did not like to be kept cooped up in the castle all the time. She would sneak out to the market or wander in the woods.

The brother of The Wicked Child fell instantly in love with her, and she with him (as often happens in kingdoms like that one). Their love broke the curse he had been under for so many years.

He dropped to his knees, praised her beauty, and begged to be forgiven for all the wicked things he had helped to do.

They talked and talked and talked until dawn. At last, he told her of his Wicked sister and how he could not return empty handed or she would know something had happened.

And thus it was that the Princess gifted him the sticky bun - the very sticky bun that would be the undoing of some and the fortune of others.

The Wicked Child's brother and the Princess continued to see each other in secret, slipping out at night and whispering their love vows. But the trees of the forest were twisted and repeated the whispers, and soon The Wicked Child heard their words.

One morning she went to her brother and asked, “Do you love me dearly brother?” Her brother answered “Always!” (as he always had).

Then she asked, “Always upon always and forever upon forever?”

And her brother replied, “Always upon always and forever upon forever!” (as he always had).

Yet, the Wicked Child was still not happy and she asked, **“Best upon best of anyone ever?”**

Her brother was dismayed, for his heart had been turned good and true by loving the Princess, and he could not lie. So he remained silent.

Then The Wicked Child looked upon him and knew he loved another more. She stamped her foot and cried,

“So, the trees do not lie! You love another more! Then I shall go out into the world and do something wicked!”

And so saying, she snatched up her rattle and ran into the woods, laughing her wicked laugh.

The Wicked Child's hair stood on end in anger.

The Wicked Child's wild eyes darted every which way, searching.

The Wicked Child's mouth grinned its most wide and wicked grin.

She ran here and there. She cursed the rabbits. She cursed the flowers. She cursed the grass.

She searched high and low for the one who had stolen her brother's heart. Then she remembered her brother liked to go to the overgrown garden in front of an old cottage where wild roses grew. (This was the same cottage the three Princesses had lived in many years before.) And woe! For the lovely Princess was waiting there now!

The Wicked Child's brother had also run into the woods and got to the old garden first. He begged his love to flee, but she would not leave him - for her love and her faith were as pure as the whitest of feathers.

And so, The Wicked Child found them there.

“You stole him!” She screamed at the Princess. Then danced about, shaking her rattle high and low in such a rage as never before.

Her brother jumped in front of the Princess to protect her, and both of them twisted in pain from the curse being cast upon them!

The Wicked Child’s brother cried out, and with the sound of his cries the rattle broke into a hundred tiny pieces.

Then The Wicked Child’s brother and the Princess became two large rose bushes that intertwined to grow and be together forever.

The Wicked Child was furious, for her rattle was broken and the Princess had still gotten her brother in the end! She stamped her feet and screamed screams upon screams! She cursed and swore with such words that all about the kingdom people covered their ears in fear. All to no avail.

Finally, she threw herself at the two rose bushes, planning to tear them to pieces. But the rose bushes were stronger than she, (for they were made and bound by pure and honest love). They scratched and pricked again and again her until all her venom-filled blood, from that serpent so very long ago, bled away.

The Wicked Child collapsed in the rose bushes, at last at peace. She would never be wicked again.

In the end, it was The Wicked Child's prank on the royal messenger that eventually brought about the birth of the very Princess who claimed her brother's heart. Each wicked act led, little by little, to her undoing. Let this be a lesson to all those who would do wicked things:

What goes around... comes around...
it just might take awhile.

Family Tree

River Kingdom
Edge Kingdom
King
Queen
Messenger
Princess
Daffy
Knight
Prince
Prince
Prince
King
Princess
Forest Kingdom
Princess
Princess
Princess
Prince
The Brother
Princess

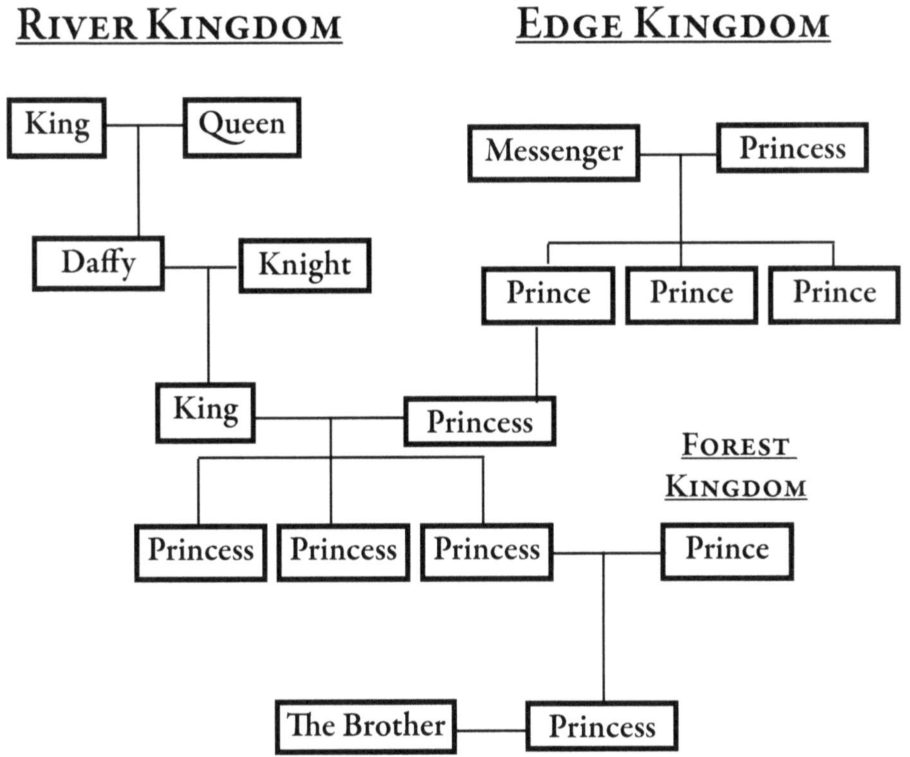

About the Author

Jessica Cathryn Feinberg is a driven, quirky, creative gal who resides in Tucson, Arizona with a house full of books, cats, dragons, and art supplies.

Jessica has been fascinated by goblins and other fae since she was very young and has dedicated her life to writing, drawing, painting, and following in the footsteps of mysterious magical creatures.

She is best known for her dragon, clockwork, and wildlife artwork as well as her field guides to rare creatures.

For more information, events, books, and to become part of monthly creations visit Artlair.com

www.ingramcontent.com/pod-product-compliance
Ingram Content Group UK Ltd.
Pitfield, Milton Keynes, MK11 3LW, UK
UKHW020422250726
13967UKWH00007B/2764

9 781647 648367